Guy Gilchrist's
JUST IMAGINE
A Book of Fairyland Rhymes

A GOLDEN BOOK • NEW YORK
Western Publishing Company, Inc., Racine, Wisconsin 53404

MY TEDDY BEAR TALKS

My teddy bear, he talks to me!
He does! He really does!
He's certainly the most talkative bear
there ever, ever was.
But don't ask him to talk to *you*,
because you won't hear a sound.
My teddy bear, he talks to *me*…
but not when you're around!

THE KINGDOM OF SCHMOO

Once upon a time in the Kingdom of Schmoo,
ruled a very loud king and he lived in a shoe.
The king's shoe was lovely—the most royal of
places,
With big bright red windows and loud giant laces!
But the dear Queen of Schmoo was much quieter and
meeker.
She just tiptoed around in her palace of sneaker!

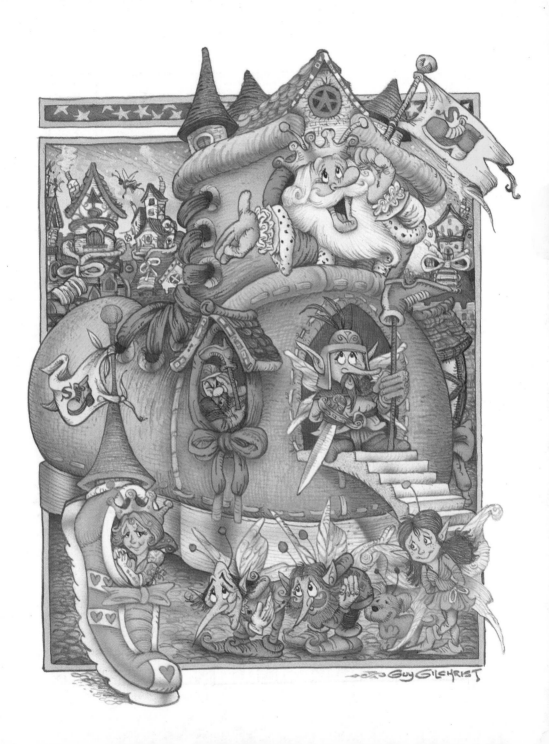

A SUMMER SHOWER

The Meadow's always wet with rain
after a summer shower.
Water dances on the blades of grass
and puts a shine on every flower.
And I lay down in the field of green
and feel the sunlight on my clothes.
I close my eyes because the sky's so bright,
the tall grass tickles at my toes.
The sounds of summer are around me now,
birds and crickets, pixie laughter…
If I could stay right here, you know I would,
dreaming happily ever after.

WINTER'S COMING ROUND

The squirrels and raccoons have made their homes,
in the trees and on the ground.
The branches of the great white oak are bare,
the fallen leaves are gold and brown.
Here come the magic frosties—
the old north wind's little men.
Time to put on my snowshoes,
winter's coming round again.

BIXIE THE PIXIE

There once was a pixie named Bixie,
Who could juggle while whistling Dixie.
And on top of all that,
He pulled cards from his hat—
Boy, I'll tell you that Bixie was tricksy!

SHOES-TOO-TIGHT FLOYD

If I were you I would avoid
A goblin named Shoes-Too-Tight Floyd.
Floyd's mom got him shoes
That were only size twos,
But Floyd's a size eight…and annoyed.

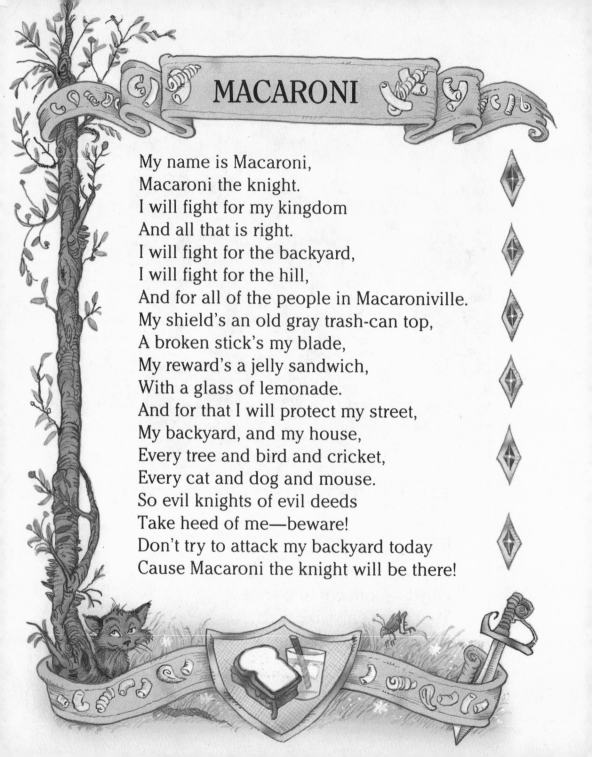

MACARONI

My name is Macaroni,
Macaroni the knight.
I will fight for my kingdom
And all that is right.
I will fight for the backyard,
I will fight for the hill,
And for all of the people in Macaroniville.
My shield's an old gray trash-can top,
A broken stick's my blade,
My reward's a jelly sandwich,
With a glass of lemonade.
And for that I will protect my street,
My backyard, and my house,
Every tree and bird and cricket,
Every cat and dog and mouse.
So evil knights of evil deeds
Take heed of me—beware!
Don't try to attack my backyard today
Cause Macaroni the knight will be there!

HARK! THE HUNGRY CAMEL

Hark! The hungry camel sings
Sugar pies and jelly rings!
Pop-see-cles and pop-see-dooses
Twenty-seven chocolate mousses!
Strawberry rhubarb and lemon meringue,
He gobbles it all with a burp and a bang!
He gobbles it all with a chomp and a chump!
Now you know it's not water he keeps in his hump!
And his hump's not filled with lunch,
And his hump's not filled with dinner,
It's filled with desserts and it never gets thinner!

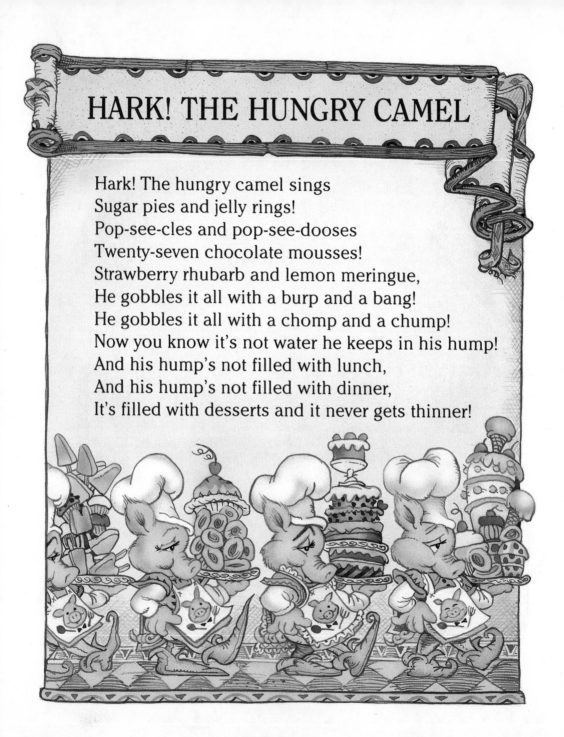

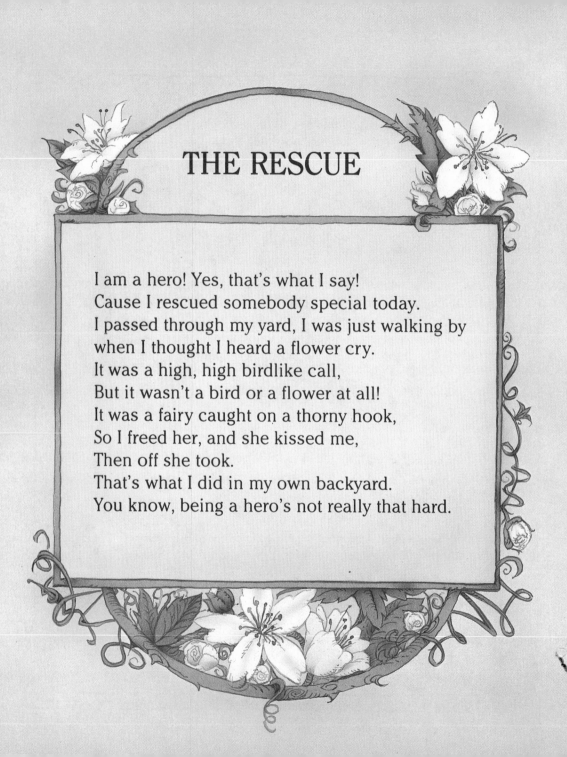

THE RESCUE

I am a hero! Yes, that's what I say!
Cause I rescued somebody special today.
I passed through my yard, I was just walking by
when I thought I heard a flower cry.
It was a high, high birdlike call,
But it wasn't a bird or a flower at all!
It was a fairy caught on a thorny hook,
So I freed her, and she kissed me,
Then off she took.
That's what I did in my own backyard.
You know, being a hero's not really that hard.

THE DRAGON'S BIRTHDAY

Call the royal cook!
Say it's time to bake.
It's the dragon's birthday.
Quick! Make him a cake!
Make it with chocolate
And honey and fruit,
Vanilla and pudding
And frosting to boot!
Bring it to him on a
Plate with gold handles
And yell "Happy Birthday!"
When *he* lights his candles!

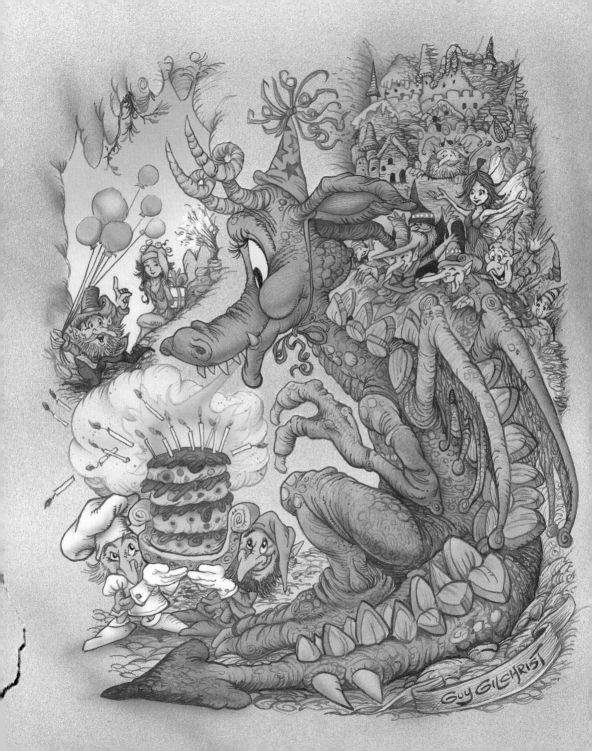

GO TELL THE KING

Go tell the king that his robe's way too long.
Go tell the king that his socks are on wrong.
Tell him his pants are the wrong shade of red,
Tell him his crown is too big for his head!
Tell him his hair should be painted bright blue.
Tell him he looks nice just wearing one shoe!
Go tell the king that his beard's made of hay.
I'd tell him myself, but I'm busy today!

FAIRYLAND SKIES

He looked out his window
From the foot of his bed.
He watched and he wondered
At the stars overhead.
Could it be that these stars,
With their bright golden glow,
Are the very same stars
That shone down long ago
On the fairyland heroes
And the maidens they loved?
Could they be the same stars
that still twinkle above?
I think they might be,
for once it was said
by a king most old and wise,
"I am but a child to the endless, ancient skies."
So maybe these stars **are** the very same stars
that twinkled long ago…
Then he went to sleep to dream the dreams
that only children know.

GOOD NIGHT

SLEEP TIGHT

GUY GILCHRIST